DATE DUE

NOV 2 8 2011			

THE OMEN AND THE GHOST

BY JOHN TOWNSEND

ILLUSTRATED BY KELLEY CUNNINGHAM

Librarian Reviewer
Marci Peschke
Librarian, Dallas Independent School District
MA Education Reading Specialist, Stephen F. Austin State University
Learning Resources Endorsement, Texas Women's University

Reading Consultant
Elizabeth Stedem
Educator/Consultant, Colorado Springs, CO
MA in Elementary Education, University of Denver, CO

STONE ARCH BOOKS
Minneapolis   San Diego

First published in the United States in 2007
by Stone Arch Books,
151 Good Counsel Drive, P.O. Box 669,
Mankato, Minnesota 56002
www.stonearchbooks.com

First published by Evans Brothers Ltd,
2A Portman Mansions, Chiltern Street,
London W1U 6NR, United Kingdom

Library of Congress Cataloging-in-Publication Data
Townsend, John, 1955–
    [The Messenger]
    The Omen and the Ghost / by John Townsend; illustrated by
Kelley Cunningham.
    p. cm. — (Shade Books)
    First published: London: Evans Brothers Ltd., 2005 under the title
The Messenger.
    Summary: On a snowy Christmas Eve, Chris ignores a series of
warnings to take a dangerous motorcycle ride with Angela, a new friend
who may be more than she appears to be.
    ISBN-13: 978-1-59889-353-3 (library binding)
    ISBN-10: 1-59889-353-X (library binding)
    ISBN-13: 978-1-59889-448-6 (paperback)
    ISBN-10: 1-59889-448-X (paperback)
    [1. Supernatural—Fiction. 2. Angels—Fiction. 3. Motorcycling—
Fiction. 4. Snow—Fiction.] I. Cunningham, Kelley, 1963– ill. II. Title.
PZ7.T66368Ome 2007
[Fic]—dc22
                                    2006026877

Art Director: Heather Kindseth
Graphic Designer: Kay Fraser

1 2 3 4 5 6 12 11 10 09 08 07

Printed in the United States of America

TABLE OF CONTENTS

Chapter 1

THE OMEN

The first warning came with the snow. The holiday lights on the tree flickered in the wind. They danced and spun. By noon they flashed on and off. Too bad they weren't supposed to.

"It looks like snowflakes got in the wires," a woman said at the bus stop. "Not a good sign."

Heavier snow swept in by early afternoon, and darkness was already crawling through the streets.

Late Christmas Eve shoppers dashed around, snapping up the last bargains. That's when the lights fizzed for the final time. The tree seemed to take its last breath. With a buzzing and popping, its lights died.

Chris brushed the dusting of snow from his motorcycle. He put on his helmet and nodded to his coworkers as they left the warehouse.

"Have a good one. See you next Tuesday," he said.

His bike coughed to life.

He pulled on his gloves and moved off in a hiss of steam and blue smoke.

He passed the dark, swaying Christmas tree and heard the piercing notes from a solo trumpet on a store's loudspeaker.

Suddenly a flurry of snowy wind shook the tree from top to bottom. The huge glass star on the very top twisted and turned on its flimsy branch. It swayed and suddenly drooped forward. It seemed to hang in the air for a second before it fell into the street, smashing to the ground just in front of Chris's wheel. Hundreds of splinters of glass burst on the street with a crash. Chris screeched to a stop as slivers of glass fell in front of his tire.

A small woman standing by the road gasped. "If that isn't an omen, I don't know what is. It's a warning to you, young man."

She looked directly into Chris's eyes. "You must beware."

She picked up a large fragment of glass. It was one of the star's points.

She handed it to Chris. "Take this, quick,"
she said. "It's a warning."

Chris held the glass in his gloved hand.

"Saved by the star," the woman said,
pointing to his helmet.

Chris smiled.

Angela had given him the helmet after he left his at his dad's. It was bright red with a gold star on the front.

"To protect you on your travels and to make you look a little special," she had said.

She'd been right about that. No other helmet looked quite like it.

With the star piece still in his hand, Chris revved the engine and went on his way.

"Beware of omens," the small woman called after him. "They come to warn us."

Omens? What did she mean? wondered Chris as he zoomed out of the town square, and splashed through the puddles.

Chris wiped wet spots from his visor as he turned onto Second Street.

He stopped outside the shoe store and waved to Angela, who was on tiptoe in the window.

She was trying to reach a shoe on display that was covered in silver tinsel and glitter. The lights flashing over her head made Chris smile.

Chris got off his motorcycle. He looked for a garbage can to throw the broken star point into. But a strange feeling stopped him from moving.

He felt like he shouldn't throw it away. He just couldn't bring himself to let it go.

The woman's words came back to him and seemed to echo in his head.

"If that isn't an omen, I don't know what is. It's a warning."

Chris looked up at the dark sky. A cold wind began to blow. A sudden shiver went through his bones. He felt uneasy. Carefully he placed the broken glass in the case on the back of his motorcycle.

An omen, he thought. To warn me about something. But what?

Chapter 2

ANGELA

Angela looked exhausted.

"What a day!" she said, sighing. "All the old men came in to buy slippers at the last minute. Typical."

Chris smiled. "I got your slippers yesterday. Pink and fluffy with purple spots. I hope you'll like them. They were on sale!"

Angela waved an empty shoebox at him. "If anyone gives me slippers for a present, I'll scream."

Chris laughed. "Can you leave work yet?" he asked.

Angela looked down. "I don't think I can go out tonight, Chris. I have to get everything ready for the after-holiday sale."

"That's too bad," Chris said. He looked disappointed. "I was going to ask you to come with me to my dad's house. You could ride on the back of my motorcycle."

Angela touched his hand. "Chris, I don't think you should go. Not on your own, in this weather. It's not safe. Please don't go, Chris."

"I have to deliver their presents. I'll be fine," Chris said.

Angela thought for a while. "Okay. I'll come with you. I'll just come in early tomorrow. I'll be outside my house at six thirty."

"We'll have Christmas Eve dinner with my dad," Chris said. Angela smiled and winked at him.

Chris had met Angela the week before at his eighteenth birthday party. Angela's band was playing at the coffeehouse where his party was. After their set, they had started talking and met a couple of times since then. She sang on weekends with her two friends.

Their band was called Omen. They were good, too, and were recording a CD. Angela looked out through the window with its blinking string of lights. "I'm not happy about the weather," she said.

"It'll be all right," Chris said. "It's supposed to get warmer tonight. Rain tomorrow. Too bad, really. Snow would be great for kids. We've never had snow on Christmas Day."

"Fifty years ago we did," said an old man clutching a pair of red slippers. "It was exactly fifty years ago that we had the coldest day on record. Not many folks remember now, but I do. The snow lasted for weeks. It was bitter cold. You youngsters wouldn't remember."

"Should I wrap those up for you?" Angela asked. She took the slippers from the man and smiled.

* * *

When Chris arrived at Angela's house that night, she was already waiting in the street, holding her sister's yellow helmet.

The road was covered in slush and puddles.

"See? I told you the snow wouldn't last," Chris said.

He had a few presents in the storage case on his motorcycle. "Keep your eye on these presents when we go over the bumps, okay? Make sure that lid on the storage case doesn't pop open."

Angela climbed onto the back as Chris's cell phone beeped.

He squinted at the text message. "7335 4U. Weird. I wonder what that means. I don't recognize it at all. Must be a wrong number."

Angela held on tight as Chris started his motorcycle. They roared down the street.

In half an hour they hoped to be at Chris's dad's house. But the weather wasn't what Chris had planned.

Just past the church, where the road began to snake across open country, it started to snow again. It was blown by an icy wind into deep drifts. It wasn't a night to be out driving.

Chapter 3
THE HAPPY HITCHHIKER

"I think we should turn around!" Angela shouted above the roar of the motorcycle. "You can't see the road."

"It'll be all right," Chris said. "This won't last long. It'll thaw soon."

Chris tried to sound sure, but the cold sliced through his gloves and coat like a blade.

He had never tried to drive in weather like this.

He felt the wheels slip and spin on the road. The beam from the headlight was useless in the driving snow. It was hard to breathe in the freezing wind.

After crawling along at five miles an hour, Chris stopped his motorcycle. "It's no good. I can't see the road. It's hopeless. We'll have to go back."

"We should have done that ten minutes ago. I told you, didn't I?" Angela said. She was already shaking with cold. She could hardly speak.

"How was I supposed to know it would get worse?" Chris said angrily. He propped the motorcycle on its stand.

"Look. There's a sign." Angela pointed at a board, lit dimly by the headlight. It said "The Happy Hitchhiker Hotel. 1 mile."

Chris went over to the sign to brush the snow off to see what else it said. There were no other words, just a picture of a smiling hitchhiker.

It was a funny old man with a plump, round face and wire glasses. Chris squinted through the falling snow.

The hitchhiker seemed to be staring right at him.

There was suddenly an eerie quiet. Chris turned around. His motorcycle sputtered as the engine died. He ran back to Angela.

"What did you do? What happened?" he shouted.

"Nothing. It wasn't me," Angela replied.

"It's never cut out like that before," Chris said. The engine refused to start. It just wouldn't spark to life. The wheels and frame were caked in snow. Ice gripped the tires.

Chris's numb fingers fumbled over his cell phone. "I'll call my dad to come get us," he said.

He held the phone in front of the headlight as he tried to make the call. "It's no good," he said. "It's dead. No signal."

Then the headlight began to flicker. The beam slowly faded. Chris and Angela stood, helpless, as the blizzard swirled around them and darkness closed in.

Above the howling wind, Angela shouted, "I think you should put your bike at the side of the road and we can walk to the hotel. We'll have to follow the telephone poles to stay by the road."

Chris's eyes lit up. "That's it! Telephone poles. I bet there's a phone booth somewhere along this road. Let's find it. I can tell Dad where we are. We need a flashlight."

He looked in the motorcycle's storage case and tore paper from one of the presents.

"This was for Barry, my brother. We need it more," Chris said.

He switched on the flashlight. It wasn't very bright, but it was better than nothing. Chris and Angela linked arms, and very slowly began to make their way through the snowy night.

Chapter 4
THE PHONE
BOOTH

Angela and Chris walked on through the snow in silence.

The flashlight only gave off enough light to see their feet.

They had to squint through the flying snow to follow the telephone poles.

"I'm sorry," Chris muttered after a while. "I was a little grumpy back there."

"It's okay," Angela said, squeezing his hand. "I told you we'd be all right. Look."

Ahead of them, standing like a lighthouse above stormy seas, was a phone booth covered in snow. Faint light glowed from the bulb inside.

Chris pulled the door open and they huddled inside. The glow from the light and the instant relief from the stinging wind made even a phone booth seem cozy. It was a relief not to feel the wind on their faces.

Chris turned off the flashlight. "I don't believe this. It's like a museum in here. It's an old type of phone. I bet it won't even work." He picked up the receiver and put his ear to it. "It's dead. Nothing."

Then Angela saw a light moving through the snow. At first, it seemed like a distant star. It shined faintly through the blizzard and flickered across the road.

"Can you see that light?" she said. She scratched a hole through the ice on the glass. "It might be help."

"I can't see anything," Chris said. "My eyes are shut. I'm hoping this is just a bad dream."

He sat down in the corner of the phone booth and pulled his knees up to his chin.

"Don't pout," Angela said.

"I'm just mad," Chris said. "I hope my bike will be okay out there."

Angela wiped the glass again and peered out into the night. "It's a car. It looks like it's coming this way."

Chris jumped to his feet and squinted out into the night.

"Hey, you're right," he said. "In that case, I think it's time for us to catch a ride."

He ran out onto the road. Shouting, he waved his arms as a car slowly chugged up the hill, honking its horn. Its headlights swept across Chris's waving arms and lit up the snow blowing in gusts across the road.

Chapter 5
STRANGE MR. SEEL

The car stopped as Chris slid up to the driver's window. The window opened and a voice came from inside. "Do you need help?"

"We need to get back to town. Could you give us a ride?" Chris asked.

"It'll be a slow ride. The wheels slip around a little in this weather. Actually, it might help to have some weight in the back to keep her steady. Get in the passenger door and climb in the back," the driver said.

Chris couldn't believe his luck. But then he saw what an old car it was. It had snow all over the hood, but it looked light brown, and had two tiny wipers slapping across the windshield. The round headlights were perched like two eyes over the front wheels.

Chris looked down at the license plate on the bumper and was just able to read the number: SEEL 4U. He stared at it for a few seconds. He could tell Angela noticed it too.

"Are you going to get in?" the driver said.

"Yes. This is my girlfriend, Angela," Chris said as he opened the passenger door.

"You both look like you just arrived from outer space," the driver said. Chris and Angela climbed inside on the backseat, clutching their helmets.

There was very little light inside the old car, but Chris could see the driver was wearing a white coat. His round wire glasses gleamed. He had a plump round face topped with thin, white hair. Turning, he held out a hand and said, "Pleased to meet you. Seel to the rescue. I'm on the way to see a friend in the hospital."

Chris shook his icy hand and smiled. "Thanks for stopping. Great license plate with your name! SEEL. Very cool."

"Yes!" Mr. Seel said happily. "This car's my pride and joy."

He pushed the gear stick with a grinding noise and the car jumped forward. The engine whined as they began to creep uphill. It was freezing inside the car and their steamy breath covered the windows.

Angela smiled at Chris. "I told you it would be all right. Oh no, I think I left the flashlight in the phone booth."

The car rocked and swayed along the twisting road. Mr. Seel leaned forward to squint through the misty windshield. "It's better with some weight in the back," he said. "She holds the road a little tighter. I hate nights like this."

Chris wiped the window to peer out. He couldn't see anything. "How old is this car?" he asked.

"1949," Mr. Seel said. "Not so old. I haven't had her long. I'd have had her a lot longer if I'd listened. It always pays to listen. I tell you, if it weren't for these telephone poles on the side of the road, I would get lost. Things are bad out there tonight."

Chris took his phone from his pocket. He looked at the last text message: 7335 4U.

He looked up at Angela. She was just staring out into the snow.

Something strange was going on. Everything seemed so unreal.

The old Dodge rumbled along. Chris could see a few lights outside as the car began to speed up. It looked like they were coming to the outskirts of town.

Mr. Seel looked into his rearview mirror at Chris.

"Well, Chris," he said, "I expect this will be a night to remember. Is it all right if I drop you off at the traffic lights?"

"Yes. Thanks a lot. That's great," Chris said.

The car came to a halt and streetlights shined through the windows.

"Back to the real world," Mr. Seel said. He smiled. He turned and looked at Chris. "Just remember SEEL 4U."

"Oh yeah, I'll remember this car!" Chris said, smiling.

"Not just the car," Mr. Seel said.

"What?" asked Chris. He was confused.

"Have a great night," said Mr. Seel. "And be careful out there."

Chris felt strange. What was Mr. Seel talking about? He started to feel dizzy. He just wanted to get out. He pushed the front seat forward, turned the door handle, and climbed out in a hurry, saying, "Thanks a lot."

Angela followed. Mr. Seel called after her,
"Good night. It's been a pleasure meeting
you, my dear."

With a slam of the door, a grinding of
gears, and a puff of blue smoke, the old car
moved away from the curb.

A little arrow lit up on the side of the car as it turned down a side street and disappeared from view. Angela waved as Chris sat on the curb with his head down, looking into a puddle. "Are you all right?" she asked Chris.

"I just feel a little sick. I hate riding in the back. And that guy was a little weird. I feel a little hot."

Hot? How strange was that? He looked around him. The streets were wet. There was no snow in sight. A mild wind blew the trees in the small town square.

"There's no snow here at all. It's really warm. Amazing," Angela said.

Chris lifted his head. "It's more than amazing, Angela. It's weird. But not as weird as that Seel guy. He was creepy. Did you feel his freezing hand and see his eyes?"

He shook his head. Then a thought came to him. "Oh no! I left my helmet and phone in the back seat of the car."

"That's the least of our worries," Angela said. "You're back safe and sound."

They stood and walked through the town. Chris looked up at the town hall clock. It was only eight o'clock. It seemed so much later.

"Come on, let's get a coffee," Angela said. "You'll feel better."

Chapter 6
GRANDMA ARELLA'S STORY

Inside a small coffeehouse, Chris stared into his coffee cup.

"Chris, you seem so down in the dumps," Angela said.

"It just doesn't make sense. It's all so strange. That weird ride," Chris replied.

"Listen, if anyone can cheer you up, my grandma can. She's only a couple of blocks away. Do you want to come?" Angela asked.

Chris soon found himself ringing the doorbell of Latimer Care Center. A sign read "Assisted Care for Senior Citizens."

"Hello, Grandma," said Angela as they entered her room. "This is Chris. How are you feeling?"

Chris was pleasantly surprised. Angela's grandma seemed like a lively old lady with lots of sparkle. He recognized her from somewhere. He knew her face. Maybe it was just that she looked like Angela.

"Chris, this is my grandmother, Arella," Angela said.

Arella brought out some rolls and coffee, and they sat on the sofa to chat.

"This even beats a meal at the Happy Hitchhiker," Chris said, laughing.

"The Hitchhiker?" Angela's grandma looked serious. "There was a terrible fire there, about fifty years ago tonight. It was awful. My grandfather was staying there that night. That's his picture up on the wall."

Chris looked up at an old brown photo of a young man's face. He stared at it for a while, wondering where he had seen the face before.

"The hotel was packed," said Arella. "In the middle of the night the rooms filled with smoke. Grandpa ran through the hallways trying to wake everyone up. He blew a trumpet that hung in the bar. He banged on all the doors. But no one heard him.

"By morning most of the place had burned down. He saved one man by carrying him out through the flames as the ceiling fell around him. But for everyone else, it was too late. His warning was ignored."

Arella went on. "And then another tragedy hit that town. Fifty years ago tonight." She sighed. "Mr. Seel was a wonderful man."

Chris looked up, choking on a roll.

"Mr. Seel?" he asked.

Arella nodded. "I was his housekeeper at the time. He insisted on driving to visit a sick friend in the hospital. I begged him not to go in that snowstorm. I tried to warn him. But he set off in his little old Dodge.

"Another car skidded across the ice and slammed him into a drift. They found them all the next day, up near the crossroads where the phone booth is. The three young men in the other car were all frozen to death. Mr. Seel was in a coma, but he was safely wrapped in a thick blanket.

"He recovered in the hospital and later moved away. He died many years later at a very old age. His name was Christopher too," Arella finished, looking at Chris.

The roll fell from Chris's hand.

* * *

"This is all so crazy. I don't know what's real and what isn't," Chris said. He was very jumpy as he walked with Angela through the town. "Tomorrow I'm going back to get my motorcycle and take a good look around."

Angela turned, gripped his shoulders, and looked him straight in the eyes. "No. Chris, don't go. Don't do that, please. It's dangerous. I'm warning you. Like my grandma once did. Like her grandpa, too. Don't do it."

"Well, we'll see about that. Come on, I'll walk you home," Chris said.

"I'll be fine." Angela kissed him on the cheek and smiled. "Be good. Remember my warning." She waved as she crossed the street. Then she melted into the night.

Chapter 7
LOOKING FOR ANSWERS

Chris couldn't sleep. He was confused and scared. Who had given them a ride? What had really happened last night?

As soon as it was light, he decided he would get his mom's bike and ride up there to find his motorcycle. He had to make sure it was safe and still there. He needed to put his mind at rest. He just had to find out if last night was real.

And then there was Angela. He wanted to see her and apologize for being moody.

At breakfast he told his mom he was going out to see a friend. She wasn't happy, but he grabbed her bicycle from the shed and rode off down the road.

Although he'd never been inside Angela's house, he knew where it was.

He knocked on the door. When a woman opened it, he said, "Good morning. Can I see Angela, please?"

"Who, dear?" the woman replied, looking confused.

"Angela," Chris said.

"There's no one named Angela here," the woman said.

"Angela. She works at the shoe store. She's in a band. I'm her boyfriend, Chris. She's my age and—"

"No, dear, I'm sorry. No one like that lives here. Sorry. I have to go check on my turkey."

Chris stood on the doorstep for a while after the woman closed the door. He couldn't believe it. He decided to go and see Angela's grandma to check the address.

Within minutes, Chris was ringing the doorbell at Latimer Care Center. An old man appeared. He was wearing a sweater and holding a newspaper.

"Hi, can I speak to Arella, please? The lady who lives in apartment six."

"No one lives there," the man replied. "It's been empty for weeks. A new woman moves in next week."

Chris couldn't believe his ears. This was crazy.

He started to doubt his own mind and memory. What was going on? He needed to go find his motorcycle and prove last night really happened.

He wanted to check something else, too. Had Angela's grandma lied to him? He needed to find out if the Happy Hitchhiker hotel really did burn down fifty years ago. He needed to find the truth.

It was hard work bicycling up the long hilly road, but he kept on. Not a flake of snow was in sight. It seemed like a different world from the place they had been the night before.

At last, in the middle of what seemed to be nowhere, Chris saw his motorcycle in the ditch. He ran over to where it stood, just as he had left it. He looked in the storage case.

The presents were still inside, but he couldn't see the piece of the broken glass star.

He tried to start the engine. It started on the first try. He'd take the risk of riding it without a helmet.

The sign for the Happy Hitchhiker stood at the side of the road. But it looked nothing like it had the night before.

This one was new, with a picture of a smiling cowboy on it.

He saw the phone booth. He looked inside.

It wasn't like the old phone booth he remembered. But the flashlight on the floor was the same. It was the exact flashlight he'd used the night before. He picked it up, jumped onto his bike, and rode toward the Happy Hitchhiker.

Chapter 8
CRASH

At the hotel, loud music blasted from every speaker. Chris looked around and spotted an old man sitting alone. Chris walked over and sat down with him.

"Do you know the history of this place?" Chris asked.

"Not a lot," the man said. "It goes back many years. It's had different names. It's only been called the Hitchhiker for about fifty years. since it burned down on Christmas Day."

"Why did they change the name when it was rebuilt?" Chris asked.

"They say a mysterious stranger appeared in the night with the snow," said the man. "He warned everyone the place was about to burn down. No one paid attention, and they were all killed, except one man.

"Then the stranger disappeared. It was very unusual," the man said.

He went on. "They recently painted a new sign with a cowboy. Trying to be funny, I suppose. I don't care for it myself."

Chris smiled.

The man pointed and said, "There's the newspaper from fifty years ago up on the wall. It tells you the name of the fellow he saved. Christopher someone-or-other."

Chris went over to read the news story. It was just like Angela's grandma had told him.

Chris returned to the old man and asked, "I heard something about a car crash, too. A Mr. Seel?"

The man took a thoughtful sip from his glass.

"Yes," said the man. "His housekeeper warned him not to go out in the storm. Fifty years ago exactly. I remember it well. Terrible weather. Bad crash. Three young men killed. They found Seel alive in a blanket. Someone must have kept him warm and safe. I remember watching them tow away his smashed car."

"The car? Where did they take it? Where is it now?" Chris asked.

"Oh, I don't know. Junkyard, probably. Yeah, that's it. It went to O'Hare's place at the other end of town. His father used to run it. He was superstitious. He'd never do anything with cars that killed people," the old man explained.

"They got it locked in one of the old sheds," the man said. "O'Hare never got rid of stuff. The car's probably still there!"

Chris left the hotel and got onto his bike. He was sure now that he hadn't imagined things last night.

Maybe he wasn't going crazy after all. But how did Angela fit into all of this?

He remembered her last words to him. "It's not safe to go up that road. Don't do it."

Her face filled his thoughts as he rode back down to the crossroads. He would go home and think about all of this. He'd try again to find Angela. Then he would go to O'Hare's Junkyard.

Just to see.

Chris was planning it all in his mind as he sped past the phone booth, so he didn't notice the sports car taking the curve too fast. He didn't see the car heading straight at him at full speed. He didn't see it swerve at the last minute to miss a young woman who appeared out of nowhere. He just saw it hit his front wheel before he was hurled into the ditch and the world went black.

Chapter 9
THE GHOST'S CAR

It was two weeks before Chris left intensive care. He had been in a coma for days. There was always a nurse by his side, and no one knew for sure whether he would pull through.

If the sports car had hit him full on, he would have been killed instantly. The police said he was very lucky.

A witness said, "That car turned at the last second. It was amazing!"

After two weeks, Chris could see visitors.

The first thing Chris said to his brother, Barry, was, "Sorry about your flashlight, Barry. It's a little bit used! But listen, I need to tell you something. You need to help me."

Chris had started to remember what had happened. He told Barry the whole story. He described Angela. What had happened to her? He asked Barry to try to find her.

"I have to see her again," Chris said. Barry promised he'd try.

* * *

Barry called the shoe store, but no one knew anything about Angela. He asked at the coffeehouse about the band. They'd never heard of Omen.

"Can you do something else for me?" Chris asked Barry a few days later. "Can you check out O'Hare's Junkyard? See if they remember the old Dodge. It's worth a try. Just let me know I didn't dream all this in my coma."

The sign swung in the icy wind: "O'Hare's Junkyard."

The junkyard looked like a bomb site
to Barry. There was junk everywhere: old
tires, tin tubs, dented fridges, and the rusted
remains of hundreds of cars. A skinny cat ran
from behind a pile of smashed baby strollers.

Barry thought it was hopeless. Why would
they have an old car from fifty years ago?
And even if they did, how would he find it?
The place was a mess. He turned to leave.

"Hey, what do you want?" someone called.

Barry turned back around. A man in overalls came out from a shed, wiping oil from his hands.

"Hi. My brother asked me to come in and see if you had an old Dodge."

"What if I do?" the man asked.

"He could make you an offer," Barry replied.

"You're talking big money for one of them. Is he a hot rod racer?"

"No," Barry replied.

"That's all right then. It's wrong to use the old models for racing. They need restoring. I'd do it myself, but I don't have time. There's an old brown Dodge rotting away in one of the back sheds."

"It's one of the cars my old man wouldn't touch," he told Barry. "It was in a fatal crash. It's all rusted up and chewed by rats now. Not worth the time."

"Can I take a quick look?" Barry asked. "Just in case."

The man shrugged. "You won't see much. It's dark in there. The car is in the last shed. You'll have to give the door a hard shove." He turned back to his work.

The door did need a shove. It only opened partway, but Barry managed to squeeze inside.

It was dark and dirty. Barry switched on his flashlight. In front of him he saw the rusted body of an old Dodge.

He spotted the dirty license plate: SEEL 4U.

The driver's door was missing, so Barry shone the flashlight inside.

Cobwebs clung to the steering wheel and dust covered everything. But there was something on the backseat.

He climbed inside. He couldn't believe what he saw.

It was a red helmet with a gold star on the front. Beside it on the seat was a cell phone.

It had a number on it. 7335 4U. Barry picked it up and put it in his pocket.

When he turned the cellphone over, the numbers looked like letters.

SEEL.

The flashlight gleamed on something shiny under the driver's seat.

Barry leaned closer and saw that it was a piece of broken glass. It looked like a piece of star.

Suddenly Barry felt cold and dizzy. It seemed as if a freezing hand had touched his forehead.

Chapter 10

A GIFT FROM BEYOND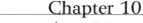

Chris woke up in the middle of the night. He'd been dreaming about the old Dodge again. He stirred, and for the first time the pain in his broken leg was no more than a dull ache.

The familiar hospital smells reminded him where he was. He felt safe. Every night he'd been aware of the nurse sitting at the end of his bed.

He opened his eyes to smile at her, but the chair was empty. A small package wrapped in shiny paper sat on its cushion.

There was just enough light that Chris could see his name on the package. Dreamily, he walked over and picked it up.

He peeled off the paper and squinted at the CD in his hands. He read the title in a daze. Omen. The CD cover showed a snow scene and the three smiling faces of the members of the band. Angela was one. Another was the young face of her grandma. The third was a man, the man in the old brown photo.

Chris lay back on the pillow with a sigh.

Still in a daze, he closed his eyes. What did it mean? Angela, Mr. Seel, Grandma Arella. They had all been there to distract him, to keep him off that road. To keep him in town. To keep him from getting into that accident. Even the falling glass star had been an omen to warn him. And the blizzard that had come out of nowhere had tried to keep him off that road.

Maybe there were protectors in the world. People whose job it was to protect others. But Mr. Seel was dead, right? Chris still felt confused.

Echoes drifted down the hallway.

Voices whispered outside his door.

Chris recognized the doctor's voice saying, "Hello, nurse. Everything all right?"

"Fine, thank you, doctor," a woman's voice replied.

"Have I seen you before? What's your name?" the doctor asked.

"Angela."

Chris opened his eyes and lifted his head.

The doctor pushed open the door to Chris's room. "Are you new here, Angela?" the doctor asked.

"Not really. In fact, this is my last night. I'm going now. My work is done."

The door swung shut. All Chris could see through the glass was her white uniform shining under the light. Then she turned with a smile and disappeared forever into the night.

ABOUT THE AUTHOR

John Townsend has been in teaching for 25 years, and has been a full-time writer since January 2003. He has written more than sixty books for young people, on such wide-ranging subjects as monsters, urban legends, spiders, computer crime, and spies. He has also written the recent thrillers *The Hand* and *Hunter's Moon*. He lives in England.

ABOUT THE ILLUSTRATOR

Kelley Cunningham has wanted to be an artist for as long as she can remember. After art school, she worked as an advertising art director, then went back to her first love, illustration. She has illustrated many books for children, as well as book covers and pieces for magazines. Kelley lives with her three sons, Sam, Noah, and Nathaniel, and their cat, Ivan, in Pennsylvania. In her spare time she is an art director in children's publishing.

GLOSSARY

bitter (BIT-ur)—very cold

coma (KOH-muh)—a person may go into a coma after an accident. During a coma, a person is in a kind of deep sleep and cannot wake up.

drift (DRIFT)—a large heap of snow

intensive care (in-TEN-siv KAYR)—a section in a hospital where people are treated for the most serious injuries

misty (MIS-tee)—foggy; when the air is full of water droplets and things look fuzzy

omen (OH-mun)—a warning that something will happen in the future

squint (SKWINT)—to almost close your eyes when you look closely at something

text message (TEKST MESS-ij)—information sent on a a cell phone

tragedy (TRAJ-uh-dee)—a sad or terrible event

whine (WYN)—to complain or make a screaming moan

DISCUSSION QUESTIONS

1. This story is called *The Omen and the Ghost*. Who or what do you think Mr. Seel is? A ghost? An alien? A visitor from the future? Something else? What about Angela and her grandmother?

2. Chris and Angela accept a ride from Mr. Seel during the snowstorm. Do you think it was wise of them to do this? Do you think it is a good idea to accept rides from people you do not know? Explain.

3. When Chris is in the hospital, he tells his brother Barry all about the strange Mr. Seel and his car. Barry promises to go hunt for the car. Why do you think Barry does this?

Writing Prompts

1. Chris and Angela stay inside a phone booth to protect themselves from the snowstorm outside. Have you ever been in a storm of any kind? How did it feel? How did you stay safe? If you weren't in a storm, imagine that you are trapped in one. Describe it, and don't forget to tell how it sounds and how you feel.

2. Chris wonders if there are secret people in the world who go around protecting others. Would you want to be one of those protectors? Write a story where you have to protect someone and tell how you do it. Remember, you have to protect them in secret, without them knowing that you are helping them.

MORE
SHADE BOOKS

Hunter's Moon
by John Townsend

STONE ARCH *Mystery*

Neil is scared, but he doesn't know why. Not at first. The dark never bothered him before. But something dangerous is lurking in the woods. Something with terrible claws. Then Neil looks up at the evening sky and remembers the mysterious message: Beware the Hunter's Moon.

Take a deep breath
and step into the shade!

Sammi and Jak are thrilled when Chad takes them on
a trip to explore a new planet. Then disaster strikes and
they are stranded, surrounded by deadly spear plants! If
only they could get back to their ship.

INTERNET SITES

Do you want to know more about subjects
related to this book? Or are you interested
in learning about other topics? Then check
out FactHound, a fun, easy way to find
Internet sites.

Our investigative staff has already sniffed
out great sites for you!

Here's how to use FactHound:

1. Visit *www.facthound.com*

2. Select your grade level.

3. To learn more about subjects related to
   this book, type in the book's ISBN number:
   159889353X.

4. Click the **Fetch It** button.

FactHound will fetch the best Internet sites
for you!